BAKERS' DOZEN

#1

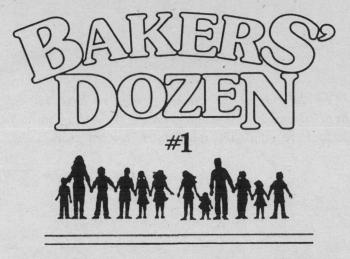

MAKE ROOM FOR PATTY

Suzanne Weyn

A
LITTLE APPLE
PAPERBACK

SCHOLASTIC INC.
New York Toronto London Auckland Sydney

To the kids at the Packer School in Brooklyn who first listened to this story. Thanks for telling me what parts were good and what parts needed more work.

With love, S.W.

ISBN 0-590-43559-0

Copyright © 1991 by Daniel Weiss Associates, Inc. and Chardiet Unlimited, Inc. All rights reserved. Published by Scholastic Inc., 730 Broadway, New York, NY 10003.

APPLE PAPERBACKS is a registered trademark of Scholastic Inc.

12 11 10 9 8 7 6 5 4   1 2 3 4 5 6/9

Printed in the U.S.A.   40

First Scholastic printing, May 1991

1

A Surprise in the Woods

EVERY ORPHAN KNOWS that almost no one adopts children older than five. And Patty Conners was eight. But someone wanted to adopt her.

In a place called Wild Falls were some people named the Bakers. They wanted to adopt Patty. That is, if they liked her.

Patty hoped that they would like her. She knew this was probably her last chance.

If this didn't work out, she might

never, ever have a real family to call her own.

Mrs. Taylor, who worked for the state adoption services agency, had picked up Patty at noon.

"At last, here's our exit," said Mrs. Taylor, turning the car off the highway.

Patty felt both excited and scared. Meeting new people made her shy. Since her mother died, she had lived in three different places. Three places in only three years.

Her first foster parents had been the Johnsons. They had a daughter Patty's age named Vera. Patty had tried making friends with Vera, but the girl kept slapping Patty. Patty took it and took it.

Then, one day, she slapped Vera back. Hard. Vera fell and broke a tooth.

That was all it took. The Johnsons said Patty had a problem getting along with other children. They sent her back to Mrs. Taylor.

After that, Patty spent four months in the children's shelter.

Then she went off to a new foster home. Mr. and Mrs. Robbins had no other children. They were nice enough, but Patty had never felt as though they really loved her.

This time, it might be different. This wasn't a foster home where you stayed for a while and then got sent away. This home would be for forever.

Patty saw a large blue sign on the side of the road. WELCOME TO WILD FALLS. They drove through town. Brick shops lined the clean, wide street.

"Do you think the Bakers will like me?" Patty asked.

"I don't see why not," Mrs. Taylor answered. "But, Patty, please try hard to make this work. No slapping. You *must* try not to be a problem."

Patty looked down. "Do you think I'll like the Bakers?" she asked.

"I think so," said Mrs. Taylor. "The Bakers are nice people. They have to be to adopt twelve children."

Patty tried not to panic. A few days ago Mrs. Taylor had asked Patty if she would mind having eleven brothers and sisters. The thought of meeting that many new kids frightened her. But she'd told Mrs. Taylor that it was okay because, more than anything, she wanted to be part of a real family.

Besides, she had told herself, *it has to be better than the children's shelter.*

That had been the worst time in her life. She'd slept on a bottom bunk in a room with six other girls. One girl told lies about her. Another tried to steal her things.

Nighttime there had been really awful. She would lie in the dark and miss her mother. Her father had left them when she was a baby. She'd never known him. But she missed her mother terribly.

Mrs. Taylor drove up a sloping road. They stopped by a mailbox with the name BAKER printed on it. Patty leaned forward. Through the trees, she saw a large gray house.

Mrs. Taylor eased the car into the long driveway. The edge of a forest came right up to the driveway. The tall trees shaded the Baker house.

It was easy to see that the Bakers had a lot of kids. A basketball hoop was mounted on the garage. A tricycle and a plastic baby car stood on the grass. A two-wheeled bike leaned against the garage door.

When Mrs. Taylor turned off the motor, they sat for a moment. The only sound was a gentle rustle as the wind blew through the forest.

Then — suddenly — *Thwack! Bam!*

From nowhere — out of the sky — a man pounced onto the hood of the car. His mouth oozed blood! His eyes bugged out of his head!

"*Aaaaaaaaaaaaaaaaaaaaaaaaaaaaaah!*" shrieked Mrs. Taylor.

2

A Weird Welcome

MRS. TAYLOR FLUNG open the car door and leapt out. Cautiously, Patty stepped out on the other side. They stared at the body lying on the hood.

"It's a dummy," said Patty.

She was right. The man on the car was made of newspaper stuffed into a white shirt and brown pants. His head was a full-sized rubber mask. Eggshells had been stuck through the eyeholes. A close look told Patty that the blood was only ketchup.

A rope around the dummy's neck was tied to a thin broken branch. Patty looked up at a tall tree near the driveway. "I think he came from up there," she said.

Just then a girl wearing red plaid pants and a yellow shirt ran out from the side of the house. She had very black skin. Her pretty, dark eyes took in the dummy, and then moved to Mrs. Taylor and Patty.

"You're going to get it now, Kenny!" the girl shouted at someone up in the tree.

The leaves rustled, and a head popped out from behind a thick branch. A short, stocky boy of about eight started to climb down. He had lots of dark wavy hair and light brown skin. "It was a mistake, Collette," he said. "I was hanging it from the tree and the branch broke."

"That was extremely dangerous, young man," Mrs. Taylor scolded. "Wait till I tell your mother!"

7

The boy looked at Mrs. Taylor for a second. Then he dropped lightly to the ground and bounded off into the woods.

"You come back here, Kenny," Collette yelled, and she dashed into the woods after him.

Mrs. Taylor turned to Patty. "He gave me a fright, that's for sure," she said, laughing nervously.

Patty wondered if those were some of the Baker children. She peered into the shadowy woods, but they had disappeared. When she turned back, Mrs. Taylor was already walking to the door.

Patty grabbed her denim backpack from the car and ran to catch up. The front door opened before they got to it. A woman in the doorway smiled and waved at them.

She had thick, honey-blonde hair clipped loosely on top of her head. She was not too tall, or too short, and she was not fat, just a little plump. "Hello,

hello," she said. "I'm so glad to meet you, Patty. I'm Ann Baker."

So this was going to be her new mother!

Patty was suddenly seized with a great shyness. She wanted to hide behind Mrs. Taylor. But that would be too babyish.

"Your son almost scared us to death," Mrs. Taylor said. She told Mrs. Baker what had happened. Mrs. Baker's eyes flashed.

"That wasn't meant for you," she said to Patty. "My kids always play silly tricks on one another."

Mrs. Baker led the way into the living room. All the furniture looked a little banged around. The low wooden coffee table had a long gash. The blue couch sagged slightly in the middle.

Patty liked the room. She could easily imagine reading a book on that sagging sofa. Mrs. Robbins had never let her put her feet on the couch, not even in socks.

Somehow Patty knew the Bakers didn't have rules like that.

"Mrs. Taylor has told me so much about you," said Mrs. Baker, sitting on a big red chair. Patty took a seat beside Mrs. Taylor on the couch. "I know you like coconut custard pie. Your favorite color is blue. Naturally, I know that you're eight, and you'll be in the third grade this September. I've registered you for school already."

Mrs. Baker paused. She seemed to be waiting for Patty to say something about school. Patty nodded, but she couldn't think of anything to say.

"Have you ever lived in the country before?" Mrs. Baker asked.

Patty shook her head.

"Patty's quiet at first," said Mrs. Taylor. "But I know she'll start talking as soon as she feels comfortable."

Patty wanted to die. She hated it when adults spoke about her as if she weren't there. They did that all the time at the children's shelter.

Mrs. Baker smiled kindly. "You must be very tired, sweetheart. That was a long ride," she said. "I have to go over something with Mrs. Taylor. Let's get you settled in. Then we can get to know one another."

Mrs. Baker rose and walked to the doorway. Patty got up and followed her slowly. Suddenly she didn't want to leave Mrs. Taylor. Once she left, Patty would be all alone among these strangers.

"Good-bye, Patty," said Mrs. Taylor. "You remember everything I've told you. This is a lucky break for you. Now you make it work."

"I will," Patty answered. She stood there looking at Mrs. Taylor. She couldn't get her feet to move.

The two women were waiting for her. "Come on, hon," said Mrs. Baker.

Patty forced her right foot to step

forward and follow Mrs. Baker up the stairs.

"Your room is on the third floor," Mrs. Baker told her. "You'll meet everyone at suppertime. They're all running around outside right now."

They climbed more stairs. Then they walked down a long hall. Patty liked the cheerful flowered wallpaper. It seemed very old-fashioned. "Your room is right down here," Mrs. Baker continued. "You'll be sharing it with — "

Mrs. Baker cut herself off. They had reached the bedroom. The door was shut tight and there was a sign taped on it. Written in red crayon, the sign read: DO NOT ENTER! STAY OUT! NO NEW KID ALLOWED!

3

Horrible Hilary

MRS. BAKER RIPPED down the sign and rapped hard on the door. "Hilary?" she called angrily. No one answered. She opened the door anyway.

Inside the room were two beds, and on one of them sat a girl with long brown hair. She wore a pink leotard with matching pink tights. An open book lay in front of her.

"Hilary, this is Patty," Mrs. Baker said to the girl.

"Hello," said Patty.

Hilary gave Patty a mean look.

"Hilary, why did you put up that sign?" asked Mrs. Baker. "You knew Patty was coming. We've talked about it all week. That wasn't a very nice way to greet her."

The girl looked at her fingernails. They were painted a bright pink. "I was practicing my ballet steps," she said, still studying her nails. "I didn't want to be disturbed."

"I didn't hear any music," said Mrs. Baker.

Hilary nodded toward a Walkman lying on the foot of the bed. "I was wearing that," she said.

"I see," said Mrs. Baker. She studied Hilary carefully for a moment and then turned back to Patty. "This is your bed." She patted the empty twin bed. It was covered with a red quilt.

Two tall dressers stood side by side. "You can put your things in this

14

dresser," Mrs. Baker said. She looked at Hilary with a worried expression. "Please make Patty feel welcome," she said. "You girls are both the same age. I'm sure you'll have a lot in common."

"I wanted to practice more," Hilary objected.

"Hilary!" said Mrs. Baker sharply.

"Oh, all right," sighed Hilary.

Mrs. Baker smiled at Patty. "See you in a little while." Then she left.

Hilary put on her headphones and began dancing to the music that only she could hear.

For a moment, Patty watched Hilary dance. Then she opened her pack. She pulled out two sweaters and took them over to her dresser. But when she opened the drawer, it was jammed with clothes. "Oh, sorry," she said, "I thought this one was mine."

Hilary didn't seem to hear Patty. She was busy bending and twirling around the room.

Patty pulled out a drawer in the other dresser. It was also full. "I thought one of these was mine," Patty said, shouting, so Hilary could hear her over the music.

"This is *my* room, and these are *my* dressers," Hilary shouted back, still dipping and rising.

Patty couldn't argue with Hilary. She didn't feel like this was her room.

Just then, someone knocked on the door. A girl who also looked about eight entered. She had short dark hair and glasses. "Hi, I'm Olivia," she said to Patty. "You must be Patty."

Finally! One of the Baker kids was being nice to her. "Hi," Patty said with a smile.

"What do you want, Olivia?" asked Hilary. She had stopped practicing.

"You know what I want," snapped Olivia. "I want my sweater that you borrowed without asking."

"Why do you think *I* have it?" Hilary asked.

16

"Because Collette saw you take it," Olivia insisted. "You are always borrowing my stuff. It drives me crazy!"

"You look horrible in that sweater," said Hilary. "Pink looks pukey on you."

"I don't care what you think, Hilary! Give me my sweater."

"You won't need a sweater in outer space," said Hilary.

"Until I get to outer space, *I want my sweater*," Olivia shouted.

"Okay, space-face, I'll get your stupid sweater. I left it in the bathroom," cried Hilary, storming out of the room.

Oh, great, thought Patty. *A Baker kid finally seems normal — and it turns out that she thinks she's going to outer space!*

Olivia looked at the open dresser full of clothing. "Boy! You unpacked fast."

"I didn't," Patty told her. "That's all Hilary's stuff."

Olivia laughed. "You mean that's the stuff Hilary has *borrowed* from everybody else."

17

"I guess," said Patty. "One of those dressers is supposed to be mine. I'm going to tell Mrs. Baker that Hilary won't empty it."

"I wouldn't," Olivia warned.

"Why not?" asked Patty.

"Rule number one is no tattling. If you want to fit in, you'd better keep your mouth shut," said Olivia. "You'll have to get Hilary to move her stuff yourself."

Olivia spotted something in the open dresser. "My new tights!" she cried. She began fishing through the drawer. "And my socks. I'm going to *kill* that Hilary. And my bunny slippers. I can't believe she borrowed those!"

Patty watched her dig. "What did Hilary mean about you going to space?" she asked.

"Oh, yes. I'm going," Olivia answered seriously. "I can't wait. It's so beautiful. There are zillions of stars and — "

Suddenly a strange sound filled the air!

"Yodel-ay-heeee-hoooooo!   Yodel-ay-heeeee-aiiiiii!"

Patty's eyes went wide with alarm. "What was that?" she asked.

4

Supper, Baker Style

"THAT'S SUPPER, " said Olivia.

Hilary returned from the bathroom. "Here's your old sweater," she said, throwing it at Olivia. Like Olivia, Hilary didn't seem at all worried about the sound they had just heard.

"Better not be late for supper," Olivia told Patty.

Hilary and Patty followed Olivia down the hall. "You have to fight for your food around here. It's like a jungle," Hilary said.

"Shush up, Hilary," Olivia scolded. "It is not like a jungle."

"Is too," Hilary insisted.

Hilary stopped near the stairs and let Olivia go on ahead of them. "Want to know what that sound was?" she whispered to Patty. "That was one of the kids being boiled for supper. The Bakers have to keep adopting new kids because they eat them."

Patty knew Hilary was lying. "That's not true," she said.

"See for yourself," said Hilary, heading down the stairs.

"Very funny," Patty muttered as she followed Hilary.

Hilary ran ahead of Patty and disappeared into the kitchen. Suddenly the strange sound came again. *Yodel-ay-heeeee-hooooooooooooo!*"

A short woman stepped out of the kitchen doorway. She was old, but she wasn't dressed like the old people Patty had known. She wore jeans and a sweatshirt, and her short, curly hair was an odd peachy color.

The woman cupped her hands to her mouth. *"Yodel-yodel-ay-heeaaaiiiiii!"* she called again.

The sound seemed to get right into Patty's head. She wrinkled her nose. The woman noticed and laughed.

"Like my yodeling?" she asked. "I learned it in Switzerland last month."

"It's very nice," said Patty politely. She had *never* been asked to comment on yodeling before.

Just then, two boys ran in from the front door. One was thin with short dark hair. His thick glasses had slid halfway down his nose.

The other boy looked younger. He had a face full of freckles and lots of reddish curls on his head. Both of them were very dirty. They stared at Patty as they passed her.

"You must be Patty," said the woman. "I'm Grannie Baker, Tom's mother. I'm always here for supper when I'm not traveling. When you hear me yodel, that's the signal to come running for the eats."

A small, delicate girl with white-blonde hair ran into the hall from the living room. She wore denim overalls and had a green ballerina's tutu on her head. She was about three years old.

"There's my Dixie," said Grannie Baker fondly.

"No, I'm Cinderella," Dixie stated seriously. "You be the stepsister. Say, 'Cinderella, get my dress!'"

"Cinderella, get my dress!" Grannie Baker said in a crabby voice.

Dixie stamped her foot. "No! Get it yourself!" she shouted. "I'm not the maid!"

Grannie Baker chuckled. "Very good, dear," she said. "Don't let anyone push you around." Dixie grinned and went into the kitchen.

"She's a modern Cinderella," Grannie

Baker told Patty. "Come and eat. You'll starve here in the hall."

Grannie Baker stepped back into the kitchen. Patty stood in the doorway and saw Mrs. Baker at the stove. Some kids were already eating. Others stood by the stove holding bowls. As each kid approached, Mrs. Baker ladled stew into his or her bowl.

A plastic, red-checked cloth covered a long table in the middle of the large room. Two large baskets overflowed with rolls. There were pitchers of juice, water, and milk, and a pile of forks, cups, spoons, and napkins.

Mrs. Baker looked up and noticed Patty. She stopped spooning food. "Everybody! This is Patty, your new sister," she announced.

Patty blushed as everyone stared at her. "Hi," said a teenaged girl. Her dark eyes were heavily lined and she had long brown curly hair. "I'm Chris."

"Hey, remember me?" cried the girl

named Collette. She was the one Patty had first seen in the driveway. "I smacked Kenny good for scaring you."

"You didn't even touch me!" shouted Kenny.

"Did, too," Collette insisted.

"Collette, Kenny, please," Mrs. Baker said.

"Sorry," said Kenny.

"Me, too," said Collette. "But Kenny started it."

"This is Olivia, Mark, and Terry," said Mrs. Baker.

Patty smiled at Olivia. The girl smiled back. Hilary sat next to Olivia, glaring at Patty. Patty looked away quickly.

Mark was a tall, Asian boy who sat slouched at the table. He held his hand up in a greeting. "Like, cool, man, another Baker," he said. "Now we have an even dozen."

"It's nice to meet you," said Terry, a girl with curly blonde hair. That's what she meant to say. It came out, "*It-th nithe* to meet you," since she was missing her two front teeth.

"You, too," Patty said, smiling.

"And this is Kevin and Howie," Mrs. Baker went on.

Howie was the thin boy with glasses. He adjusted his glasses and studied Patty. "Most interesting," he said to the red-headed boy. "We will have to study this further."

"It might be an enemy agent from the planet Zemor," the smaller boy suggested.

"Don't be so rude," Chris scolded. "Howie and Kevin never stop playing," she told Patty. "I think they're super-hero secret agents today."

"Ninja heros from the planet Nimnim, if you don't mind," Howie corrected Chris.

"Whatever," said Chris.

"These are the littlest Bakers, Jack and Dixie," Mrs. Baker finished.

Dixie sat at the table with her ballet tutu still on her head. Beside her was a pudgy boy of about five with light brown skin and large green eyes. Jack smiled and wiggled his fingers at Patty.

Patty smiled back. She knew it would take awhile before she remembered all the names.

She looked around for Mr. Baker. Just then a very tall man came through the kitchen door. He had wispy blond hair. His tan jacket was a little too short in the sleeves. "Sorry I'm late," he said.

"Hey, Pop!" Mark shouted.

"Hey, son," said Mr. Baker.

At that moment Dixie reached across the table and accidentally knocked over the whole pitcher of milk. "Yow! It's dripping all over me!" cried Kevin, the boy with curly red hair.

The milk was everywhere! Everyone jumped up and mopped it with towels and sponges.

"Jack, don't do that," Mr. Baker said as the five-year-old sopped up milk with his striped shirt.

Arf! A large black dog appeared from under the table. "Most fascinating. Jojo has milk all over him!" said Howie, pushing his glasses up his nose.

Milk dripped down Jojo's forehead. He barked and shook his head.

"Come here, Jojo," Terry called to the dog. "I'll *wath* you off." Jojo jumped up and put his front paws on the table. But his right paw slid in the milk. One of Jojo's nails hooked onto a small rip in the cloth.

"Uh-oh!" cried Dixie. Jojo was pulling the tablecloth right off the table!

"Jojo! No!" cried Grannie Baker. As the dog jumped about excitedly, he pulled the entire cloth down with him.

Smash!

Bash!

Everything fell!

The pitcher of juice. The water. The bowls full of stew.

Patty stepped back and watched as things crashed and rolled onto the floor.

Jojo barked and ran around the table trying to get free of the cloth. The rip had turned into a tear and Jojo's paw had gone completely through it. He dragged the long cloth all over the kitchen.

Mrs. Baker and Grannie leapt toward the dog at the same time. They smashed into one another. "Owww!" they cried, rubbing their heads.

Now Mr. Baker tried to get Jojo. "Calm down, boy," he said. Then he slipped on a piece of stew meat. Bam! He hit the floor. "Darn it, Jojo!" he shouted as he sat up.

Finally, Mark grabbed Jojo. He held the dog and stroked him. "Chill out, Jojo," he said soothingly. "Everything's cool."

Jojo settled down as Mark petted him. Soon Mark was able to lift the cloth off Jojo's paw.

"Good work, Mark," said Mrs. Baker, still holding her head. Mr. Baker was bent over, his hands on his back. The kitchen was a wreck.

"What's that smell?" asked Chris.

"Oh, no!" cried Mrs. Baker. "The stew is burning."

Patty backed out of the kitchen. How could Mrs. Taylor have sent her here? This wasn't a home. It was a nuthouse!

5

The First Night

ALL THE BAKERS HAD finally cleaned up the mess in the kitchen. Patty and Grannie Baker sat alone together at the table, making peanut butter and jelly sandwiches for anyone whose dinner had been dropped or burned. Mrs. Baker was upstairs putting warm towels on Mr. Baker's back. He had hurt it when he fell. All the other kids had gone off to the den or the living room or their bedrooms.

Patty was glad not to be with the

31

Baker kids. There were too many of them. And only one of her. At least there was only one Grannie Baker. Patty didn't feel so outnumbered.

Grannie handed Patty a sandwich. "Eat yours now before the thundering herd of Baker kids returns to gobble it all down," she said. "I'll pour you some milk."

"How come Mr. and Mrs. Baker adopted so many kids?" Patty dared to ask.

"Well, my brother Horace had no children and he always liked Tom — that's Mr. Baker." Grannie stopped and frowned. "Don't call him Mr. Baker. Call him Dad."

"But I hardly know him," Patty objected.

"I see your point," said Grannie Baker. "Call him Tom then."

I couldn't, thought Patty. She never called adults by their first names.

"Anyway," Grannie continued, "Horace died and left a large sum of money to Tom. Tom is a teacher at Wild Falls College. Now, no one ever got rich teaching, although it's a fine profession. But, suddenly Tom had all this money. Tom and Ann — that's Mrs. Baker — had always wanted kids, but they weren't able to have any of their own. The doc didn't know why. Sometimes it just happens that way. So, when Tom inherited all that money he said to Ann, 'Let's use this money for something really important. We'll adopt us a big, happy family.' So they did."

Patty took a long gulp of the milk Grannie had given her. "How come they adopted so *many* kids?" she asked.

"They just like kids, I guess," Grannie answered. A smile formed on Grannie Baker's face, as if she had just thought of something funny. "Now that you've come, they have an even dozen kids," she said. "And since our name is Baker, we could call you kids a baker's dozen.

Although twelve really isn't a baker's dozen."

Patty looked confused. "I don't understand."

"In my day, if you bought a dozen rolls from a baker, the baker threw in the thirteenth roll for free," Grannie Baker explained. "Thirteen of anything came to be known as a baker's dozen."

"I'm glad they don't have thirteen kids," said Patty. "I think twelve is plenty."

"Don't be so sure there won't be thirteen," said Grannie. "You never can tell what the future will bring."

Just then, Mr. Baker walked into the kitchen.

"How are you doing, Tom?" Grannie asked.

"I think I pulled a muscle," he said, sitting on a chair next to Patty. He held out a large hand to her. "I'm Tom Baker. Pleased to meet you."

Patty took his hand. Her own hand

disappeared inside it as they shook. "Pleased to meet you, too," she said, smiling shyly.

"Sorry things were so crazy today. But they're pretty crazy every day," he told her. "Are you all settled in upstairs?"

Patty thought about the dresser filled with clothes. She could tell him about that now. But she remembered Olivia's warning and just nodded.

"Great," he said, getting up. "Ready for the picnic tomorrow?"

"What picnic?" asked Patty.

"The Wild Falls teachers and staff picnic," he told her. "Lots of hamburgers and corn-on-the-cob. It happens every year. If we don't get rained out, it should be great."

Patty looked out the window. It was pouring.

He headed toward the kitchen doorway. "Excuse me, but I have to lie down. My back is killing me," he said. "Everything okay down here, Mom?"

"Sure thing," Grannie told him.

Later that evening, Mrs. Baker showed Patty to the upstairs bathroom. Patty showered, gathered her things, and headed for her new bedroom.

Hilary was already there, dressed in a flowered nightgown with ruffles down the front. She sat on the floor putting together a puzzle. She looked up when Patty came in and then went back to her puzzle.

Patty took a hairbrush from her pack and began brushing the damp tangles from her strawberry-blonde hair.

"Cut it out!" cried Hilary. "You're spraying water all over my puzzle."

"Sorry," Patty said. She stepped away from Hilary and went back to brushing.

"I said stop it!" Hilary shouted. "A drop landed on me!"

Patty narrowed her green eyes. But she didn't say anything. She didn't want to fight with Hilary.

There was a knock on the door. Mrs. Baker stuck her head in. "Everything okay in here?" she asked. She saw that Patty and Hilary were angry. Then she noticed Patty's bag on the bed. "Do you need help unpacking?" she asked.

Again Patty remembered Olivia's words. No tattling. Despite her anger, she didn't want the others to think she was a snitch. "I'll do it tomorrow," she told Mrs. Baker.

Hilary had put away her puzzle and gotten into bed. Mrs. Baker kissed her on the cheek. "Goodnight, Hilary, dear," she said. "I know it's hard to share your room. I'm proud of you."

Hilary smiled sweetly at Mrs. Baker.

Mrs. Baker came over and put her hands on Patty's shoulders. "Do you need anything at all?" she asked.

Patty looked quickly at the dresser. "No," she said.

Mrs. Baker bent and kissed her on

the forehead. It felt so good to be kissed!

Mrs. Robbins had never kissed her. Patty hadn't been kissed by anyone in a long, long time.

After Mrs. Baker left, Patty turned to Hilary. "You'd better clear out that dresser tomorrow," she said.

"I'll think about it," said Hilary. She snapped off the light that was mounted near her bed. Then she rolled over, with the covers pulled up high over her shoulders.

Patty pulled back her quilt and crawled into bed. There was a light like Hilary's by her bed. She snapped it off.

Patty lay awake in the dark and listened to the *tap-tap-tap* of the rain against the window. She watched the narrow, curvy rivers of water run down the glass.

Soon, soft snores came from Hilary's bed.

Patty reached to the end of the bed and grabbed her pack. She dug through it until she finally found what she had been looking for. "There you are," she whispered.

6

Zanzibar Marie

PATTY SMILED AT the rag doll on her lap, and smoothed its worn blue-checked dress. Two black button eyes stared back at her. Long yarn braids stuck out from under the doll's blue bonnet. "What do you think of this place, Zanzibar Marie?" Patty asked softly.

Zanzibar Marie was Patty's dearest treasure. Her mother had made the doll. Patty remembered watching her work on it in the evenings while they watched TV together.

On the night the doll was finished, they had been watching a show about a place called Zanzibar.

"Zzzzzzan-zzzzzibar," Patty had repeated the name from the TV show. The Z's tickled her tongue. "I'm going to name my doll Zanzibar," she told her mother.

"That's an awfully long name for such a little doll," her mother had pointed out.

Patty thought about that. "I'll give her a short name, too. Marie. Zanzibar Marie."

"That's very pretty," her mother had agreed.

Patty hadn't known it then, but her mother was very sick. She went into the hospital two weeks after she finished Zanzibar Marie. She died one month later. Patty was only five.

When Patty held Zanzibar Marie, she could pretend that she was sitting beside her mother watching TV. She could almost see her mother smiling at her, tenderly brushing the hair from her forehead. Zanzibar Marie was all Patty had left of her mother.

"I don't know if I like it here or not," she whispered to Zanzibar Marie. "Mr. and Mrs. Baker are nice. And Grannie is pretty cool. But I don't know about the kids. That Hilary certainly is a big creep."

The rain still pounded on the windowsill. Patty rubbed Zanzibar Marie against her cheek. The doll had gotten sort of raggedy in the last three years, and Patty wondered what the other kids would think of her.

She loved Zanzibar Marie. But she wasn't ready to show her to the Bakers. She didn't want to take the chance that they would make fun of the doll.

Patty snuggled down under the covers and hugged Zanzibar Marie tightly. "Goodnight, Z-Marie," she said sleepily. "I have a big day tomorrow. I'm going to a real country picnic."

7

The Picnic

DURING THE NIGHT, the rain stopped. Patty was awakened by the sun on her face. Zanzibar Marie lay beside her. She pulled the doll under her covers and quickly looked over at Hilary. But Hilary's bed was empty.

There was a knock on her door. "Not up yet?" said Mrs. Baker pleasantly as she entered the room. "Hilary was supposed to wake you."

"I guess she forgot," said Patty.

Mrs. Baker wore jeans and a T-shirt.

Her hair fell loose around her shoulders. Patty thought she looked very pretty.

Mrs. Baker noticed Patty's full pack. "Why don't I help you unpack?" she asked.

"I . . . um," Patty stammered, remembering the no tattling rule.

"Come on," said Mrs. Baker. "It will only take us a minute." Mrs. Baker opened one dresser drawer and saw Hilary's things. Then she opened the other and saw that it was also full. An angry red colored her cheeks. "That Hilary," she muttered.

Mrs. Baker ruffled Patty's hair. "We haven't had a moment to give you a proper welcome," she said. "What if we have a special 'Welcome, Patty' supper tomorrow night? Would you like that?"

A special supper! "I'd like that a lot," Patty answered. No one had ever made a special supper just for her!

"Then that's what we'll do," said Mrs.

Baker. "Now you get dressed and come down to breakfast. We'll be leaving for the picnic soon." Mrs. Baker put her arm around Patty's shoulder. "I'll have Hilary empty this drawer when we get home today."

Patty got dressed. Even though she noticed that Hilary's bed wasn't made, she made hers anyway. "See you later," she told Zanzibar Marie, putting her back into her pack.

When Patty got to the kitchen, everyone was gulping down a breakfast of donuts and hot cocoa. Hilary glanced at Patty from the corner of her eye, but she didn't say anything.

"I wish we had this for breakfast every day," said Kenny. His face was covered with white powder from his donut.

"Forget it, pal," laughed Mr. Baker. "This is a special picnic-day treat."

"Can we go now?" asked Collette.

"Everybody finished?" asked Mr. Baker.

"Yeah!" the kids yelled at once.

"Okay, then. Into the van," Mr. Baker said.

The kids raced out of the kitchen. They almost knocked Mr. Baker over as he headed for the doorway.

"I'm sitting in the front!" yelled Kevin.

"Only Captain Nordica sits in the cockpit!" cried Howie, chasing him. "*I* am sitting in the front."

Patty grabbed a donut and followed the others outside. Mr. Baker helped Patty climb into the Baker's big red van.

"This picnic is going to be great," Olivia told Patty. "We went last year."

"They have pony rides," Collette added.

"Oh, whoop-dee-doo," said Hilary sourly. "You couldn't even gallop. You had to walk around in circles."

Collette shrugged. "I liked it."

"Me, too," Olivia agreed. "But the coolest thing is this big net cage with a

46

giant puffy air mattress in it. All the kids go in and jump around. You bounce real high. It's like being on the moon. No gravity. You can pretend, anyway."

"Olivia wants to be an astronaut," Collette explained.

Oh, thought Patty. *That explains this stuff about going to outer space. She's not weird after all.*

When they arrived at the picnic the family followed Mr. Baker across the parking lot and over to a large grassy area. People were putting out food on tables and grills. There was a fenced-in area with ponies. Patty saw the bouncing ride Olivia had mentioned.

They stopped at an empty picnic table. "Remember, we're right here near the hot dogs," Mrs. Baker told them all. "Stay together. I don't want anyone going off alone."

The Baker kids seemed to know

everyone. They ran in every direction as they spotted their friends. Patty had hoped that Olivia and Collette would stay with her. But she turned around just in time to see them running off with two other girls.

Hilary had also spotted a friend. The girl looked older, about ten. Her blonde hair was crimped into a frizzy style. Hilary was about to leave with her, but Mrs. Baker called her back and spoke very seriously to her.

Then Hilary walked over to Patty. "Come on," she snapped. "I have to take you with me. Mom wants us to get to know one another."

Patty looked over to Mrs. Baker. She didn't want to go with Hilary. "Go on, Patty," said Mrs. Baker. "Hilary has promised me that she's going to try to be nicer from now on."

"Come on, already!" called the older girl. Patty and Hilary joined her.

"This is Marissa," Hilary told Patty.

"Patty is the new kid I told you about. She just got here."

"Hi," said Patty.

"Hi," said Marissa, looking Patty up and down. The girls began to walk across the grass. "What's with your parents, anyway?" Marissa asked Hilary. "Don't they have enough kids?"

"Enough is not the word," Hilary agreed. "It's like a zoo."

"Guess what I heard my mother saying?" Marissa said in a low voice. "She said that your mother was an orphan. That's why she adopted so many kids."

"That's true," said Hilary.

Wow! thought Patty. *Mrs. Baker is an orphan, too. That did help explain why she adopted so many kids.*

"When my parents were alive, I was the only one," said Hilary. "I had my own room, all my own stuff."

"And then they died in a sailing accident," Marissa said dramatically. "What a romantic way to die."

Patty couldn't believe her ears. Marissa was talking about it as if it were a TV show! "How did you get to the Bakers?" Patty asked Hilary.

"None of your business!" Hilary snapped.

8

Lost!

MARISSA AND HILARY walked along, ignoring Patty. Patty wanted to leave, but she remembered what Mrs. Baker had said. No one was to go off alone.

After a while, they had walked far away from the others. They were in a quiet part of the park, near a lake. "At least I had my own room for a while," Hilary said to Marissa. "Then she came."

"I didn't ask to be in the room with you," Patty spoke up.

Hilary looked at Patty. "It doesn't matter. You're there." Hilary whispered something to Marissa. Marissa giggled and nodded.

"Marissa has to tell me something in private," Hilary told Patty. "We're going over into those trees. You wait here."

Folding her arms, Patty walked closer to the lake. What did she care about their stupid secrets? She picked up a rock and threw it into the water.

She waited. And waited. Soon she realized what they had done.

They had run away and left her there!

Tears filled her eyes. She didn't care if they were gone — but still . . . What a mean thing to do!

They might say she went off by herself. Then Mrs. Baker would be angry with her.

Maybe they were hiding. She ran into the woods to find them. "I know you're here," she called.

Patty listened. A twig snapped several yards away. She followed the sound.

She walked deeper and deeper into the woods. "Hilary!" she yelled. There was no answer.

Patty looked all around. She couldn't remember how she'd come in. She kept walking, looking for a clearing.

She walked until her legs ached. Finally she saw a stretch of flat green grass through the trees. She ran toward it as fast as she could.

When she got out of the woods, she was still lost. She had come out in a part of the park she hadn't seen before. *I'll never find my way back,* she thought hopelessly.

Then, in the distance, Patty saw a man on a horse. He saw her, too, and rode over to her. He wore a gray uniform with the words, "Wild Falls State Park Ranger," written on it. He seemed very high up as he sat on his white and brown horse. "Can I help you?" he asked Patty.

"I'm lost," she told him. "I was at a

picnic. I think it's for college people."

"The Wild Falls College staff picnic," the ranger said. He got down from the horse. "I'll take you back there." As he spoke he picked Patty up and placed her on the saddle. In a moment, the ranger was back up behind her.

"We'll go slow. I promise," the ranger said.

Patty wasn't scared. She was excited to be on a horse — even though it seemed much larger than horses looked on TV.

They rode past the lake. Soon the picnic came into view.

Patty hoped Mr. and Mrs. Baker didn't think she had disobeyed and gone off by herself.

"Where are your parents?" the ranger asked Patty.

Patty wasn't sure how to answer. Were the Bakers her parents? It felt strange calling them that. "Over there," she said.

The ranger headed the horse over to

the Bakers. Patty realized that everyone was looking at the ranger, the horse, and her.

When Mr. and Mrs. Baker spotted her, they ran over. Mrs. Baker carried Dixie in her arms. Chris, Kevin, and Howie ran along behind them.

Mr. Baker got there first. "What happened?" he asked.

"Your little girl here was lost," the ranger told him.

"Where is Hilary?" asked Mr. Baker.

"I don't know," said Patty. Mr. Baker lifted her off the horse. He thanked the ranger.

"Are you okay?" asked Mrs. Baker, looking concerned.

Patty nodded.

"Let us observe this large beast," said Howie as he and Kevin went to see the horse.

"Horsie!" cried Dixie.

Chris took her from Mrs. Baker. "I'll show you the horse, Dix," she said. A small crowd had gathered around the horse.

"Come and have a hamburger," Mrs. Baker said to Patty.

"No thanks," Patty replied. She saw a worried look in Mrs. Baker's eyes. Was Mrs. Baker thinking that Patty hadn't listened to her?

Was she thinking Patty was a problem child?

9

Patty Fights Back

FOR THE REST of the picnic, Patty stayed close to Mr. and Mrs. Baker. She wanted them to see how obedient she was.

At about four o'clock, the kids began to wander back to the picnic table. When Hilary returned she pretended not to notice Patty. Mrs. Baker noticed Hilary, though, and took her aside. Patty could see that Mrs. Baker was scolding her. *Good,* Patty thought. *I'm glad you're in trouble, Hilary!*

Soon all the children had returned. "I

rode the pony!" cried little Dixie, running ahead of Chris.

Kenny came back covered with mud.

"What happened to you?" asked Mrs. Baker.

"I got into a game of touch football with some kids," he explained.

"They must have been pretty dirty kids," Mrs. Baker laughed.

Mr. Baker counted heads. "Twelve Bakers, all present and accounted for. Okay, troops, head for the van."

The Bakers walked across the park to the parking lot. Olivia and Collette came up alongside Patty. "Boy, Hilary is mad at you," said Collette.

"What for?" cried Patty. "I should be mad at her."

"She told Mom you ran away from her and Marissa," said Olivia.

"That's a lie!" cried Patty. "She ditched me."

"Did you tell Mom about the drawers

being full?" Collette asked. "Mom says Hilary has to empty them."

"I didn't tell," Patty objected.

"That's not what Hilary said," Olivia insisted.

"Well, I didn't tell," said Patty. "Mom saw it for herself."

On the way home, Patty pretended to sleep. She didn't want to talk to anyone.

"Dixie and Jack come with me," said Mrs. Baker, as they pulled into the driveway. "You're getting baths. Then the hot water will be used up for an hour or so."

"I'm in charge of laundry this week," Chris announced. "I want everyone's dirty clothes in one pile in the hall. Mark, you help me fold."

"Aw, come on, Chris," the tall boy moaned.

"I washed the bathrooms for you last week," Chris reminded him.

That evening the Bakers had chili for

supper. Grannie Baker had made it while they were at the picnic. This time, Patty wasn't scared when she heard the yodel. Suppertime was still hard to get used to, though. The kids went back and forth from the stove to the table holding their bowls of chili.

Hilary sat at the far end of the table and didn't look at Patty once. That was fine with Patty.

After supper, Patty wandered into the den. The kids were watching TV. Everyone was there but Hilary. Patty wondered if Hilary had gone to clear out the dresser for her.

Patty looked for an empty chair, but didn't find one. There didn't even seem to be space on the floor.

"Hot water's back!" called Mrs. Baker.

She came into the den behind Patty. "Why don't you take a shower next, sweetheart," she said to Patty. "Do you remember where everything is?"

"Yes," said Patty, heading up the stairs.

Patty went first to the bedroom to get her nightgown and brush. Hilary was lying on her bed reading a *Betty and Veronica* comic. Without a word, Patty went to get her things.

Instantly she saw that her pack lay flat and opened on her bed.

"What did you do with my stuff?" she demanded.

"I unpacked it for you," Hilary answered.

Patty yanked open a drawer. Hilary's clothing was gone. Patty's clothes had been dumped inside.

Suddenly Patty's heart skipped a beat. Zanzibar Marie was not in the drawer!

She ran back to the bed and looked into her bag. The doll wasn't there. She checked under the bed. No doll. "My doll!" Patty cried. "Where did you put it?"

Hilary continued reading.

Patty crossed the room and grabbed the comic from Hilary's hands. "I said where is my doll?"

"I don't know what you're talking about," Hilary said, but there was a sly smile on her lips.

That little smile was more than Patty could take. She shoved Hilary's shoulder. "I want my doll, now!" she yelled.

Hilary pushed back. "Get your hands off me!"

In a rage, Patty grabbed Hilary's arm. She yanked her off the bed. Thud! Hilary hit the floor. In a second, Patty was on her.

Hilary grabbed hold of Patty's hair. "Owwwww!" Patty shrieked.

At that moment the door flew open. Mr. and Mrs. Baker stood in the doorway. All the kids were behind them.

"What is going on?" asked Mr. Baker.

Hilary pointed at Patty. "She attacked me — and for no reason!"

"You liar!" cried Patty. "You stole my doll!"

"That's enough," said Mr. Baker. "Hilary, do you have Patty's doll?"

"I don't know what she's talking about," said Hilary, folding her arms across her chest.

"It was in my pack. And now it's gone," said Patty.

"Are you sure you didn't leave it somewhere?" asked Mr. Baker.

"Yes. I never took her from this room. *She* has her," insisted Patty, pointing at Hilary.

"Do not," said Hilary.

"Hilary, tell the truth," demanded Mrs. Baker.

"I did not take it!" cried Hilary.

"Is that the truth, Hilary?" asked Mr. Baker.

"Oh, great!" Hilary sulked. "You believe her and not me."

"We just want to know what happened," said Mrs. Baker.

"Isn't it possible that you left it somewhere?" Mr. Baker asked Patty.

"No," Patty told him. "She was in my pack."

This was just like what had happened at my first foster home, Patty thought. Vera had slapped her until she fought back. Then, when she had defended herself, they said it was she — Patty — who was to blame. She remembered what Vera's mother had told Mrs. Taylor. "Patty has trouble getting along with other children."

Mr. Baker clapped his hands. "All right, everybody. Let's start getting ready for bed." The Baker kids followed their father from the doorway.

"Hilary, if you took that doll, you must give it back," said Mrs. Baker.

"I told you, I didn't!" yelled Hilary.

"All right, I don't know what to do then," said Mrs. Baker. "Patty, if we don't find the doll, we'll get you another. I promise. Maybe it will turn up."

"I don't think it will," said Patty.

"Come on, Patty," said Mrs. Baker. "Take your shower."

"All right," said Patty, still glaring at Hilary. After Mrs. Baker left the room, Patty took her nightgown from the drawer.

"Guess what," said Hilary. "You just showed everybody what you're really like. Now you're going to get sent back to the children's shelter."

10

The Search
for Zanzibar Marie

THE NEXT MORNING Patty woke up early. The first thing she did was look under the covers for Zanzibar Marie. Then she remembered that the doll was gone.

There was a tight pain in Patty's chest. Without Zanzibar Marie, she felt all alone. She knew Zanzibar Marie was a doll, but she thought of her as a friend. A best friend, who had been by her side no matter where she went.

Now her doll was gone. If the Bakers

66

sent her back to Mrs. Taylor, she wouldn't even have Zanzibar Marie.

Hilary was still sleeping, but Patty could hear other voices in the hall. Patty got out of bed and put on her robe. She walked out into the hall.

"Halt, ninja warrior!" shouted Kevin. He wore a pair of navy-blue boxer shorts on his head and waved a plastic sword. "I said halt, ninja!"

"I'm not a ninja," said Patty.

"Not you. Him!" cried Kevin.

Turning, Patty saw Howie in the hall-way. He had a blanket over his shoulders. He slashed the air with a make-believe sword. "I challenge you, samurai master!" Howie cried, pushing up his glasses. With a leap, Kevin chased Howie down the hall.

As she watched them disappear down the stairs, Patty realized she was starting to get used to the Bakers. They seemed strange at first. But in only a day and a half, all the craziness was beginning to seem ordinary.

Breakfast was as hectic as all other Baker meals. Mr. Baker dished out oatmeal from a large pot. Milk, spoons, and bowls were on the table, along with boxes of cold cereal. The kids crowded around the table, eating.

"Grab a bowl," Mr. Baker told Patty. He wore a blue robe over striped pajamas. His hair was mussed and he looked as if he wished he were still in bed sleeping.

Patty tried to read his face. Did he look like a man who was about to send an orphan back to the shelter? Was he angry that his twelfth kid had turned out to be a troublemaker?

No, he just looked tired. Patty decided he must be good at hiding his feelings. But she wondered if he had already called Mrs. Taylor.

Mrs. Baker stuck her head in the kitchen doorway. "Does anyone need me for anything?" she asked. Everyone kept eating. "Great," she said. "Then I'm taking a shower."

"I have to go!" cried Dixie, scooting down from her chair.

"Good girl!" said Mrs. Baker. "Let's go use your potty." Dixie hurried off with Mrs. Baker.

Five-year-old Jack sat at the table beside Patty. "She's getting toilet trained," he explained.

"That's nice," said Patty.

Hilary came down looking sleepy. When she saw Patty, she stuck out her tongue and made a face.

"Who's on garbage detail today?" asked Mr. Baker.

"Mark is," said Kenny.

"Well, get it out of here," said Mr. Baker. He pointed toward a full black garbage bag. "That bag is about to burst," he said.

Mark had been reading the back of a cereal box. He looked over at the garbage. "That's from yesterday," he said. "Kenny was supposed to take it out yesterday."

Mr. Baker rolled his eyes. "Okay, Kenny, you take out this kitchen garbage. Mark, you make a run through the house and take out all the rest," he told them.

"No fair," Mark objected. "The trash upstairs is all from yesterday."

"Mark, just do it," said Mr. Baker firmly.

All around Patty, the kids were finishing up. "Come on, Collette," said Olivia. "We have to finish reading those books on our summer reading list. School is in two weeks." The two girls put their bowls in the dishwasher and left.

Chris took Jack's hand. "Get ready to go. I'm taking you and Dixie to the early movie, remember?"

Mark got up from the table. "Want to shoot some baskets, Kenny?" he asked.

"Okay," Kenny agreed.

"Don't forget the garbage, guys," said Mr. Baker as the boys went out the kitchen door.

"Tom," Mrs. Baker called from upstairs, "would you come here a minute? I think we have a leak under the bathroom sink."

"There's always a leak somewhere in this house," Mr. Baker muttered as he left the kitchen.

Before she knew it, Patty was alone at the table with Hilary. The two girls didn't even look at one another.

Patty quickly finished eating and took her bowl to the dishwasher. She went up to the bedroom and dug through Hilary's drawers. But Zanzibar Marie wasn't there.

Patty checked under Hilary's bed and under her covers. She couldn't find the doll anywhere.

She pulled on her jeans and T-shirt. She would search the whole house if she had to.

Patty spent the rest of the morning searching for Zanzibar Marie. She looked in the living room and the den. She lifted the chair cushions and checked under the couch.

She went down to the basement. There were three large baskets of laundry beside the washing machine. Patty looked through each of them. But still no doll.

Patty went outside. She looked under the bushes near the house. Then she trudged out into the woods and searched there for a half hour. Still no sign of the doll.

Patty walked back to the house. Suddenly she remembered her welcome supper. They were supposed to have it today. That would tell her what she needed to know. If there was a welcome supper, it meant they had decided to let her stay. If not, it meant they were sending her back.

When she opened the back door, she

sniffed the air. There was no roast cooking. No spaghetti sauce on the stove. The clock on the wall said it was almost twelve, but there didn't seem to be much cooking going on for her welcome supper. In fact, there was no sign of lunch, either.

Upstairs, Patty passed the bathroom and saw Mr. and Mrs. Baker sitting on the floor. Mrs. Baker was holding onto a pipe under the sink. Mr. Baker was turning part of the pipe with a wrench. They didn't notice her as she walked by.

Olivia and Collette were reading in their bedroom. "Did you find your doll?" asked Olivia.

"No," Patty answered.

"Don't worry," said Collette. "There are tons of dolls in this house."

"It's not the same," said Patty. There was only one Zanzibar Marie.

"Make way. I'm coming through," shouted Mark. He came down the hall dragging a full, black plastic garbage bag behind him. He stopped at Collette and Olivia's room and dumped their trash into his bag. Then he went on down the hall.

"Want to borrow a book?" Olivia asked Patty. "We're supposed to read ten by the time school starts and we haven't even — "

"No thanks." Patty cut her off. She didn't have time to talk. She'd just realized something. Mark was taking out the trash. What if Hilary had thrown Zanzibar Marie into the garbage?

Once the garbage truck came, Zanzibar Marie would be gone forever.

11

The Trash Disaster

IN THE YARD two lumpy black bags of garbage sagged side by side at the back fence. Zanzibar Marie *had* to be in one of them. Where else would she be? Patty had looked everywhere.

Patty untied the wire tie on the first one. *Peeeuuu!* She had opened the kitchen garbage. It stunk. She quickly retied it.

Hilary wouldn't throw Zanzibar Marie into the kitchen garbage. There always seemed to be someone in the kitchen.

The second bag was tied in a knot on top. Patty wiggled her fingers into the knot, but she couldn't undo it.

Quickly she looked around to see if anyone was watching. Then she dug her fingers into the plastic until she'd made a small hole. Then she ripped the bag open.

Patty dug through the trash. She found old papers, ripped cardboard from opened toys, a frazzled toothbrush. There was a sock with ink stains and a broken windup toy. But no doll.

She kept digging. The more Patty dug, the bigger the hole in the bag became. Soon all the trash was in a pile by Patty's feet.

But Zanzibar Marie wasn't there.

"Uh-oh," said Patty, looking down at the mess she'd made. There was trash all around her. *Mr. and Mrs. Baker are going to kill me if they see this,* she thought.

Patty scooped up the trash. She stuffed two handfuls back into the bag.

Just then a strong wind blew through the yard. It swept up a torn comic book and sent it sailing into the yard.

She ran after the comic as it tumbled across the grass. "Got you," she said, stepping on the cover. She turned back to the torn trash bag. Her jaw dropped.

While she had been chasing the comic, the wind had blown more papers out into the yard. The mess was getting bigger by the moment. Patty ran after the blowing papers, but the wind scattered the garbage faster then she could pick it up.

"This is hopeless!" Patty cried.

At that moment, she noticed someone at the kitchen window watching her — Hilary. In the next second, Hilary turned away and was gone.

Patty's shoulders sagged. It was all over. First she'd gotten lost at the picnic. Then she had attacked Hilary. Now she'd made this huge mess in the yard.

This was strike three. When the Bakers saw this she would be out. And Hilary would make sure they saw it.

A fat tear traveled down Patty's cheek. She couldn't face being sent back to the shelter. That's what was going to happen, though. She'd been nothing but trouble to the Bakers since she'd arrived.

She had to think fast. Any minute now Hilary would lead the Bakers out into the yard.

Patty could imagine their faces when they saw their yard. They would look at her, standing in the middle of the blowing trash and think: *She's a problem child. We'd better send her back.*

Patty started to run. She wasn't sure where she was running to, but she had to get away.

Through the trees, she could see the road. She'd head for it — and keep going. Right now, the important thing was not getting sent back to the shelter.

Patty had almost reached the road

when she heard it. *Crunch, crunch, crunch.* The sound was coming from behind.

Patty froze and listened.

It was the sound of footsteps. Someone was chasing her!

12

A Serious Talk

"HOLD ON, WILL YOU!" called a familiar voice.

Patty whirled around.

It was Hilary.

Patty brushed the tears from her eyes. She didn't want Hilary to see her cry. "Leave me alone," she shouted at Hilary.

Hilary kept running toward her.

Patty was about to start running again. Then she saw what Hilary had in her hand.

Hilary was holding Zanzibar Marie.

"Boy, you made some mess back there," Hilary said, catching her breath.

"Give me my doll!" Patty said. She sprang forward and tried to grab Zanzibar Marie from Hilary's hand. But Hilary was too quick for her. She jumped back.

"Don't be so grabby!" Hilary said.

"It's mine and I want it!" Patty yelled. She was all set to jump on Hilary, knock her to the ground, and take back her doll. She didn't have to, though.

"Here's your stupid doll," Hilary said, throwing the doll at Patty.

Patty caught Zanzibar Marie. Her checked dress wasn't torn. Her braids and bonnet seemed fine. At least Hilary hadn't hurt the doll. Patty held her tight.

But what was Hilary up to? Patty wondered. Why had she returned the doll?

It didn't matter now. She would never see Hilary again.

"Where are you going?" Hilary asked.

Patty began walking toward the road. "What's it to you?"

Hilary followed her. "You're running away, aren't you?"

Patty didn't answer.

"You won't get very far," said Hilary. "Mom and Dad will call the police. They'll come pick you up."

"How do you know?" Patty snapped.

"Because I tried it," Hilary said.

Patty stopped and turned to her. "You did?" she asked. "Why?"

Hilary knelt and tied the lace of her sneakers. She didn't look at Patty as she answered. "Because I didn't think Mom and Dad really wanted me."

"Why not?" Patty asked.

Hilary looked up at her. "I was the first kid Mom and Dad adopted. When my natural parents died in the sailing accident, they had it in their will that I should come here. Mom and Dad Baker were friends with my parents."

"So?" said Patty. "You were lucky. You never went to a shelter or a foster home or anything."

"Maybe, but they didn't expect me. When I came to live with them, they were in a tiny apartment. I had to sleep on this bumpy pullout couch. I had to keep all my clothes in my bag. I just got dumped on them," Hilary recalled.

"How old were you?" Patty asked.

"Four," said Hilary.

"What did you do?" asked Patty.

"One day while Mom was on the phone, I took my suitcase and left," said Hilary. "I thought that if I could find my old house, then my real parents would be there. Pretty dumb, huh?"

Patty shrugged. "Four-year-olds always think weird things," she answered. "What happened then?"

"I couldn't find my house. Then Mom showed up. She was in a police car. They were looking for me," said Hilary.

"Things got better after that. We moved to this house and it was just the three of us for a while."

Hilary paused. "It would have been great if Dad didn't get all that money," Hilary went on. "But once they got the money, they just went crazy adopting kids. I went from having the whole house to myself to not even having my own room."

"Don't you like the other kids?" asked Patty.

Hilary shrugged. "They're okay, I guess," she admitted. "But we sure didn't need another one!"

"If you had left me alone, I would have been gone by now!" Patty said angrily.

"Maybe I should have," said Hilary. "But you looked so pitiful out there digging in the garbage. It made me feel kind of bad, so I went to get your doll. When I came down with it, I saw you running."

"Why did you chase me?" Patty asked.

"Who knows?" said Hilary. "Maybe I felt sorry for you. Maybe I remembered how I felt when I ran away. I'm not sure."

Patty looked over at the road. She realized that she didn't really want to run away. It was kind of scary not knowing where she would eat or sleep. Besides, the police probably *would* find her.

"I can't help it that we have to share a room," she said to Hilary.

"I'm getting over it," Hilary said. "I don't like it. But I'm not as mad today as I was on Friday. Maybe I won't even notice you after a while."

Patty smiled slightly. This was probably as nice as Hilary was able to be. "I guess it's hard always having to share stuff with a ton of kids," she said.

"It's the worst," Hilary grumbled. She turned and began to head back to the house. "You get used to it, though. Sometimes it's even fun. Just *sometimes*."

Patty walked along beside Hilary. Patty wasn't always so happy to share her things, either. She supposed she could understand a little of how Hilary felt.

When they got nearer the house, Patty heard voices in the yard. "They found the garbage. You're in trouble now," said Hilary. But this time she didn't seem happy about it.

Patty gulped. She thought she'd left the trash problem behind.

She took a deep breath. Might as well go face it.

Hilary and Patty stepped out of the woods into the yard. Patty was glad to see that Mr. and Mrs. Baker were not there. All the other kids were, though.

Chris stood in the middle of the yard. Her hands were on her hips. "Who did this?" she asked Patty and Hilary.

13

Some Surprises

"Jojo DID IT," Hilary spoke up.

Patty was shocked. Hilary was sticking up for her!

"Jojo was with me," said Kenny.

"I did it," admitted Patty. "I didn't mean to. I was looking for my doll."

"Did you find your dollie?" asked Dixie.

Patty held up Zanzibar Marie. She decided to let them think the doll had been in the trash. She didn't have to say that Hilary had taken it. Hilary was trying to be nice. Patty decided she would try, too.

Chris shook her head in dismay. "Come on everybody," she said. "We'd better clean up this yard before Mom and Dad see it."

Without another word all the kids began gathering the trash. Collette went inside and got another garbage bag. With twelve of them working, the yard was cleaned up in no time.

"Next time, be more careful, Patty," Chris said.

Next time. Patty liked the sound of that. It sounded as if her life here were going to last forever.

"She will be," said Hilary.

The afternoon had gotten cooler. When the garbage bag was retied, the kids went inside.

Grannie Baker was in the kitchen, spooning stuffing into four large roasted chickens. Today she wore baggy overalls over a flannel shirt. Her peachy hair was still perfectly neat.

"Hope you like chicken, stuffing, and yams," Grannie said to Patty. "Because I spent all morning making them."

The other kids kept moving through the kitchen. Patty stayed behind, gazing at the chickens. "I didn't even know you were here," said Patty.

"I wasn't. Ann called me at home. She and Tom are having plumbing problems, so she asked me to cook your welcome supper. I like to cook at home and reheat things here. It's much calmer at my house."

"This is my welcome supper?" Patty asked happily.

"Sure is," replied Grannie, her small eyes twinkling. "And you won't have to wait until suppertime, either. Ann and Tom like to eat in the afternoon on Sundays."

Patty felt as if she would burst with happiness. They hadn't forgotten her.

And they weren't sending her back!

Just then, Mr. Baker came in the back door. He held a brown bag and a large, white box. Patty could tell the box came from a bakery.

"No peeking in that box," said Mrs. Baker. She had come to the kitchen doorway, still holding the wrench she'd used to fix the plumbing.

"Maybe she could have a little peek," suggested Mr. Baker. "Since it is for her." He opened the box a crack.

Patty looked. Inside was a large coconut custard pie with the words *Dear Patty, Welcome! Love, Mom, Dad, Grannie, and all your brothers and sisters* written on it.

"It's beautiful," Patty said with a big smile.

Mr. Baker reached into his bag and took out a bouquet of daisies wrapped in pretty paper. "These are for you, too," he said. "They're from me and your mom."

Patty took the flowers. "Thank you," she said happily. "No one ever gave me flowers before."

Mr. Baker put his hand on her shoulder. "We take some getting used to, but we're very glad you're here," he said.

Patty felt all shivery happy inside. "Me, too," she said.

"You found your doll," Mrs. Baker noticed.

Patty nodded.

"Patty," said Mrs. Baker. "Try to put up with Hilary. I know she can be — "

Mrs. Baker was interrupted by the sound of someone shouting down the stairs.

"Patty, are you coming?" Hilary called.

Mrs. Baker looked surprised. "Are things between you two getting better?" she asked.

"Better," Patty said, still smiling.

"All right then, go on," Mrs. Baker said.

"I'll be yodeling in about a half hour,"

said Grannie. "So wash up. Send Olivia and Collette down to set the table. I believe it's their week to set."

When Patty got to the stairs, Hilary was at the top. "I want to move the furniture in our room around," she said to Patty.

"Okay," Patty agreed.

Hilary didn't wait for her. She hurried on down the hall.

Patty climbed the stairs. The warm smell of her welcome supper had begun to fill the house.

In the middle of the stairs, Patty stopped. She hugged Zanzibar Marie to her. "Maybe it will be okay here after all," she whispered to the doll.

Somehow Patty was sure that Zanzibar Marie agreed with her one hundred percent.

Giving the doll one more squeeze, Patty went up to her bedroom — the one she shared with her sister, Hilary.

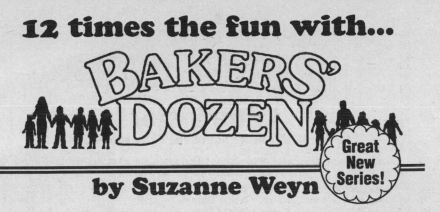